DC
COMICS™

BATMAN™

TALES OF THE
BATCAVE

THE PENGUIN'S
POWER PARASOL

by
MICHAEL DAHL

illustrated by
LUCIANO VECCHIO

Batman created by
BOB KANE WITH BILL FINGER

STONE ARCH BOOKS
a capstone imprint

Published by Stone Arch Books in 2016
A Capstone Imprint
1710 Roe Crest Drive
North Mankato, Minnesota 56003
www.mycapstone.com

STAR36189

Library of Congress Cataloging-in-Publication Data is available on the Library of
Congress website.

ISBN: 978-1-4965-4012-6 (library binding)
ISBN: 978-1-4965-4016-4 (paperback)
ISBN: 978-1-4965-4020-1 (eBook PDF)

Summary: With the Blue Diamond of Russia on display, Batman and Robin know a
super-villain's on the way. But when the Penguin drops into the Gotham City Museum,
the Dynamic Duo is surprised by the punch in his parasol. Can the Boy Wonder save the
Caped Crusader from a perilous ride atop a jet-powered umbrella? Or will the Penguin
slip away with the ice?

Editor: Christopher Harbo
Designer: Bob Lentz
Production Specialist: Kathy McColley

Printed and bound in the USA.
032017   010318R

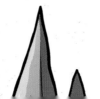

TABLE OF CONTENTS

This is the BATCAVE.

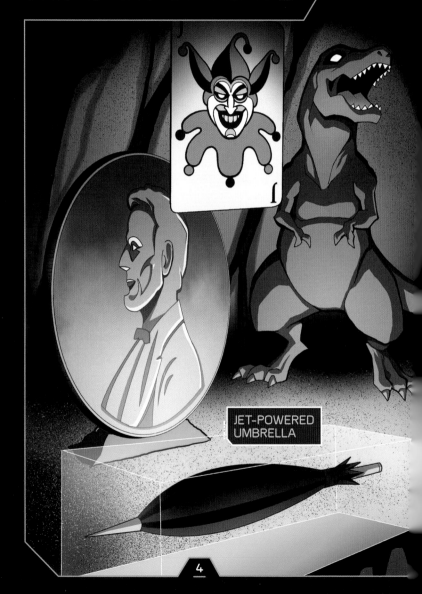

JET-POWERED
UMBRELLA

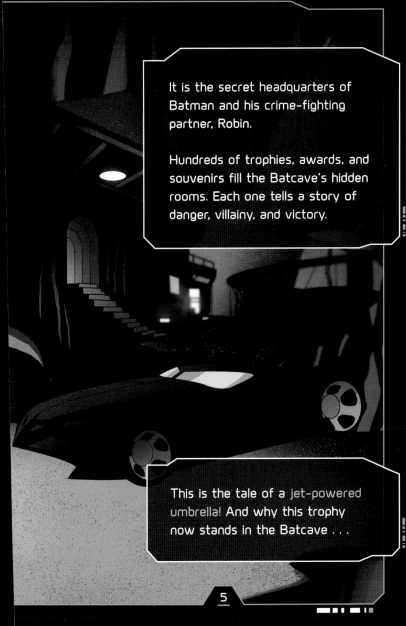

It is the secret headquarters of Batman and his crime-fighting partner, Robin.

Hundreds of trophies, awards, and souvenirs fill the Batcave's hidden rooms. Each one tells a story of danger, villainy, and victory.

This is the tale of a jet-powered umbrella! And why this trophy now stands in the Batcave . . .

CHAPTER 1

BLUE ICE

"That's some rock!" says Robin, the
Boy Wonder.

"It's the famous Blue Diamond of Russia,"
says Batman. "The world's most valuable gem."

The Dynamic Duo hides in the shadows
inside the Gotham City Museum's Grand Hall.
They secretly guard the rare diamond.

Hundreds of people fill the Grand Hall to see the Blue Diamond. The gem is locked in a glass case under a domed ceiling.

"Gosh, Batman," says Robin. "Do you really think some crook will try to crack that case?"

"He'd have to be a pretty cool customer," replies Batman, "to steal that piece of ice!"

"Of course!" says Robin, punching his glove. "Ice! The word criminals use for diamonds."

"And we know plenty of criminals who can't resist stealing a little ice," Batman says. "Mr. Freeze or —"

Suddenly, the glass dome high above the Grand Hall shatters.

Thousands of pieces of jagged glass fall
toward the floor.

The crowd screams and runs for safety.

"The Penguin!" shouts Robin.

CHAPTER 2

Playing With Fire

The pudgy Penguin floats down to the floor using his trick umbrella.

He laughs as he sees the Blue Diamond.

"Ha, ha!" the Penguin croaks. "Has everyone left you alone, my blue beauty?"

"Not everyone," says Batman. He and Robin jump from their hiding place.

"You're the one who's going to be blue," shouts Robin. "As soon as we put you behind bars!"

"I'm not going back into cold storage!"
yells the Penguin. "Things are going to
get hot around here instead!"

The villain aims his umbrella at the heroes.

The villain pushes a button on the umbrella's handle. A huge jet of flame shoots from the umbrella's tip.

"Oh, no!" cries the Boy Wonder.

The Caped Crusader hurls himself at Robin. He knocks his partner away from the roaring flames.

"Bravo," says the Penguin. "You can save your little friend . . ."

Then the villain aims his trick umbrella at a group of museum-goers standing near a statue.

". . . but can you save *them*?"

CHAPTER 3

FALL OF THE EMPEROR

The Penguin's umbrella shoots out a fearsome flame.

The hot flames hit the base of the statue.

As the base melts away, the huge figure begins to fall.

"This is terrible," says Robin.

"Indeed it is, Boy Wonder," says the Penguin. "Ivan the Terrible, to be exact. Russia's most famous emperor!"

The people near the emperor's statue scream with fear.

Batman and Robin quickly unfold Batarangs from their belts.

The heroes throw their weapons toward the falling emperor. The Batarangs whirl through the air.

Strong ropes trail behind the weapons. They wind around and around the statue.

The Dynamic Duo races up a staircase. They tie the ends of the Batarang ropes to the stair rail.

CRASH!

The base beneath Ivan the Terrible collapses. But the statue stops falling just in time.

Robin sees the diamond case is broken.

"That dirty bird is getting away!" he says.

Batman slides down the staircase railing. He leaps and lands in front of the fleeing Penguin.

The Penguin squawks with fear and drops his umbrella.

CHAPTER 4

WHAT GOES UP...

Batman steps over the fallen weapon.

"Hand over the diamond," says Batman. "You are going down!"

Suddenly, the Penguin laughs.

"And you are going up!" says the villain, pulling a remote control from his pocket.

He presses a button. The umbrella pops open behind Batman's back.

SNAP! SNAP!

Metal bands clamp around his boots and his gloves.

The handle of the trick umbrella fires like a rocket. Slowly, it rises into the air.

Batman is carried up through the broken glass dome.

"When he reaches the stratosphere, he'll freeze like an icicle," says the Penguin.

CHAPTER 5

...Keeps Going Up!

"Too bad you can't fly, little robin!" says the Penguin.

The Boy Wonder presses a button on his Utility Belt.

"Just watch me," he says.

A few moments later, a roar comes from the sky.

Robin looks up.

It is the Batplane, answering his signal.

The plane lowers a strong cable and pulls the crime fighter up.

Meanwhile, the Dark Knight grows colder.

His locked hands cannot reach his
Utility Belt.

He struggles atop the umbrella as it climbs higher and higher.

Batman can see his breath.

Icicles form on the edge of the umbrella.

The hero's hands and feet grow numb.

His lips turn blue.

Then he hears a familiar roar.

It is the Batplane!

The plane zooms closer.

The jet engines tilt and the plane hovers like a helicopter.

A hatch opens in the underside of the plane.

The umbrella keeps rising.

It rises up and up, carrying Batman through the hatch.

The hatch closes.

The umbrella pins Batman to the ceiling of the Batplane.

"Batman, are you okay?" shouts Robin, running from the cockpit.

"Up for anything now, Boy Wonder," replies Batman. "Thanks to you."

Robin finds a switch to turn off the umbrella and frees his partner.

"The Penguin got away," says Robin.

"Yes," says the Caped Crusader. "But he doesn't know I planted a tracker on the Blue Diamond."

"Brilliant, Batman!" says Robin. "The tracker will take us right to that tricky bird!"

Batman picks up the smoking parasol.

"Umbrella or no umbrella," he says, "the Penguin's crime wave is about to fold!"

EPILOGUE . . .

"The Penguin must never get his hands on this powerful parasol again, Robin."

"But what should we do with it, Batman?"

"Let's take it to the Batcave. We'll save it for a rainy day."

GLOSSARY

cockpit (KOK-pit)—the area in the front of a plane where the pilot sits

collapse (kuh-LAPS)—to fall down suddenly

emperor (EM-pur-ur)—a male ruler of an empire

hatch (HACH)—a covered hole in a floor, wall, or ceiling

numb (NUHM)—unable to feel anything

parasol (PA-ruh-sol)—an umbrella often used to shade sunlight

signal (SIG-nuhl)—a radio, sound, or light wave that sends information from one place to another

stratosphere (STRAT-uh-sfihr)—the layer of Earth's atmosphere that begins 7 miles (11 kilometers) above the ground

tracker (TRAK-uhr)—a device that allows someone or something to be followed

valuable (VAL-yoo-buhl)—having great use or importance

Discuss

1. Why do you think the Penguin likes "ice" so much?

2. Why do Batman and Robin stop the statue from falling instead of grabbing the Penguin right away?

3. Batman and Robin have special tools and equipment that help them fight crime. Can you find three of their tools in the story, and say how they were used?

Write

1. Robin uses the Batplane to rescue Batman. Can you think of another way Robin might have saved him? Write about what he could do instead.

2. Batman has placed a hidden tracker on the Blue Diamond. He and Robin will be able to find where the Penguin is hiding. Write a paragraph and describe what happens when the heroes surprise the villain.

3. Robin uses a signal on his special belt to summon the Batplane. If you had a belt like that, what could it do? Write a short paragraph describing your crime fighting weapons and tools. Then draw a picture of them.

Author

Michael Dahl is the prolific author of the best-selling *Goodnight Baseball* picture book and more than 200 other books for children and young adults. He has won the AEP Distinguished Achievement Award three times for his nonfiction, a Teachers' Choice Award from *Learning* magazine, and a Seal of Excellence from the Creative Child Awards. He is also the author of the Hocus Pocus Hotel mystery series and the Dragonblood books. Dahl currently lives in Minneapolis, Minnesota.

Illustrator

Luciano Vecchio was born in 1982 and is based in Buenos Aires, Argentina. Freelance artist for many projects at Marvel and DC Comics, his work has been seen in print and online around the world. He has illustrated many DC Super Heroes books for Capstone, and some of his recent comic work includes *Beware the Batman*, *Green Lantern: The Animated Series*, *Young Justice*, *Ultimate Spider-Man*, and his creator owned web-comic, *Sereno*.